Learning to read requires many more skills than just decoding words. This lively, colourful book is for young children who are not yet reading. It will encourage them to look closely at pictures, to spot similarities and differences, to practise sequencing and anticipation, and to enjoy the fun of 'reading' a story told in pictures.

On each double-page spread, the artist has hidden a little ladybird like this:
Can your child find it?

British Library Cataloguing in Publication Data

Picture reading.
  1. English language. Readers — For schools
  I. Lobban, John
  428.6
  ISBN 0-7214-0854-0

First edition

Published by Ladybird Books Ltd Loughborough Leicestershire UK
Ladybird Books Inc Auburn Maine 04210 USA

Printed in England

picture reading

by LYNNE BRADBURY
designed and illustrated by JOHN LOBBAN

Ladybird Books

Circus time
Talk about this picture.

How many wheels can you count?

How many clowns?

Do you know the names of these colours?

red   *green*   *blue*

Find each colour in the picture.

yellow   orange   purple

How many red things?

Look carefully at each pair of pictures.
What's different?

Which picture matches the shadow exactly?

Which comes first in each row?

Which comes last in each row?

Five teddy bears sitting on a shelf.

When one falls off there are only four.

Now look at these pictures and put them in order.

Tell the story

③

④

⑤

*Talk about the pictures in the
right order.*

Which comes last?

At the harbour
Find six differences in the picture opposite.

Count the boats.
How many men can you see?

Do you know these nursery rhymes?

Here are two endings to each rhyme.
Which one is correct?

Which of the pictures, a, b or c, comes next in the line below?

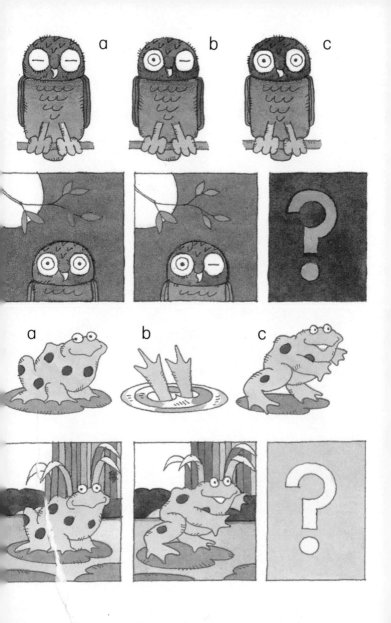

Tell the story

What has the mouse found?

What do you think might happen next?